I0640584

Firebrand Firestorm

The Ancestors of Bjorn Esterday

Volume 11

Wicked Schemes

July 1st and 2nd 1776

Wynter Sommers

Wynter Sommers

Published by Pure Force Enterprises, Inc.
California, USA
Since 2002

INGRAM
INGRAM® Distribution

DEDICATION

To those who feel strongly about truth,
justice, and the integrity of America;
your honorable actions make us proud.
To those who wonder if their daily
choices matter; your small decisions
impact generations to come.
To those everyday people who don't think
they have what it takes; when you strive
for extraordinary things, the impossible
becomes reality.
Your dreams today become our future
tomorrow.
Thank you for everything you do.

Bjorn Esterday
Was Not Born Yesterday
Series

Firebrand (15 Volumes+Conversation Station Book)
Edges (9 Stories +Conversation Station Book)
Gone (18 Stories + Conversation Station Book)

Bjorn EDGES Series

EDGES Book 1-Swift Encounter
EDGES Book 2-Rousing Attack
EDGES Book 3-One Foot Under
EDGES Book 4-Earthshake
EDGES Book 5-Broken String
EDGES Book 6-Key Witness
EDGES Book 7-Who is She?
EDGES Book 8-Vanish
EDGES Book 9-Chase or Die

Bjorn Series Alternate Reading Plan

1st	Edges Book 1		22nd	Gone Book 10
2nd	Edges Book 2		23rd	Firebrand Vol 9
3rd	Gone Book 1		24rd	Gone Book 11
4th	Firebrand Vol 1		25th	Firebrand Vol 10
5th	Edges Book 3		26th	Gone Book 12
6th	Firebrand Vol 2		27th	Gone Book 13
7th	Gone Book 2		28th	Firebrand Vol 11
8th	Gone Book 3		29th	Gone Book 14
9th	Firebrand Vol 3		30th	Firebrand Vol 12
10th	Gone Book 4		31st	Gone Book 15
11th	Firebrand Vol 4		32nd	Firebrand Vol 13
12th	Gone Book 5		33rd	Gone Book 16
13th	Gone Book 6		34th	Firebrand Vol 14
14th	Edges Book 4		35th	Gone Book 17
15th	Firebrand Vol 5		36th	Firebrand Vol15 (End)
16th	Gone Book 7		37th	Gone Book 18 (End)
17th	Firebrand Vol 6		38th	Edges Book 5
18th	Gone Book 8		39th	Edges Book 6
19th	Firebrand Vol 7		40th	Edges Book 7
20th	Gone Book 9		41st	Edges Book 8
21st	Firebrand Vol 8		42nd	Edges Book 9(End)

ACKNOWLEDGMENTS

We acknowledge those who actively build peace. We acknowledge all the selfless talent which contributed to creating meaningful tokens of consideration and sharing. We acknowledge that every person has a daily choice of right or wrong... and we thank you for choosing the right, good, honorable path filled with integrity because that is the difficult and brave path. Small choices today become lasting monuments of loving hope tomorrow.

CONTENTS

0 PREFACE

Button is waiting for the obnoxious opera singing divo[1], Henry Mossop, to show himself as he paid Mr. Tweedbottom to ensure Mossop's status in the wealthy circles of society.

Bryce Aiden Tyler leaves the Dunlap home after he gets the information he needs.

A new friend of Button's, Susanna, shows him how to slip through the secret passages to underground networks to save lives. Meanwhile Polly continues to translate the document so that more people could understand the price of freedom.

---

[1] Divo is Italian for a prominent tenor. The form of the word assigned to a female is "Diva". Another term used to indicate a starring male singer is "Primo Uomo". The female version is "Prima Donna".

1 CHAPTER 102: (JULY 1 1776) Spy Silversmith Through the Coffee Shop Window as the Chase Ensues?

Jane sat looking as this very simple, matter-of-fact woman, Susanna Wright, in the coffee shop of Meeting Town.

Out the window, she saw Silversmith still standing there.

Jane could sense that Susanna Wright was growing impatient. As Jane glanced out the coffee shop window, she was recalling how fortunate it was that Mr. Bryce Aiden Tyler and Magistrate Karl

Pinkney happened upon her broken hired carriage. They were able to transport her and her travelling companions to Meeting Town, saving her from spending a night in the wilderness.

Jane listened to Susanna Wright accurately and succinctly convey Jane's own story back to her. Jane's eyes wandered to observe the back of Silversmith, who was gazing out onto the street in front of the coffee house.

As if she needed to verify what she saw was in fact happening, Jane witnessed Mr. Bryce Aiden Tyler, on horseback, pursuing a man, who was on foot.

Then, Jane recognized the man as the opera singer, Henry Mossop.

"Pardon me," Jane mentioned to her coffee companion as she rose from her chair and swiftly made her way to the door. Susanna Wright followed her.

"Why," Jane asked aloud, "Is Uncle Floyd's business partner chasing the opera singer my Uncle was invited to watch perform?"

"I do not know, but I would wager," Susanna Wright added, "that we should investigate further, as I've had some suspicions about that fellow."

Jane was about to exit and get the attention of Silversmith, when Silversmith also started to run after them. They all disappeared around a corner.

Some other coffee shop occupants had also clustered to the doors and windows to observe this odd sight.

Then there was silence.

Suddenly, Silversmith came running back toward Jane. Alone. She stopped, leaning up against the wall of the coffee house, gasping for breath.

"Silversmith, Silversmith," Jane called with concern, "... what goes on here?" Susanna Wright silently followed behind

Jane, curious herself.

Silversmith was still gasping for breath.

Jane came closer to Silversmith and quietly asked, "What is that opera singer doing in this town? When Mr. Tweedbottom told me he had to conduct business in New York, I assumed all the men at Lady Sarah Wilson's estate would likewise return to their homes. Why is Henry Mossop still in the Colonies and why is Mr. Tyler chasing him?"

A crowd started to form around the women and Jane helped Silversmith along to a side alley, smiling to inform the onlookers that there was nothing unusual at all.

Susanna Wright helped out by announcing to the crowds, "It is simply this fine lady's maid returning from an errand. You may return to your conversations and go about your business."

Jane smiled a "Thank you" to Susanna Wright for her assistance in disbursing the crowds.

Once the crowds thinned to an acceptable number, Jane asked Silversmith again, "I see an opera singer, who should be on his way back to Ireland, chased by my Uncle's business partner, who is then chased by you... Silversmith I do require some details."

Silversmith replied, "He had to make sure Mr. Henry Mossop would not board that boat..."

"What boat?" Susanna Wright queried.

Silversmith looked at Jane as if to ask for permission to speak freely in front of this other person. Jane nodded.

"Go on," Jane prodded, "Tell us what you know ..."

Silversmith replied, "When you arrived, Miss Jane, you were exhausted and slept... both you and Miss Eliza were in your rooms all day. I hadn't time to tell you what I overheard and how Billy Dawes rescued me, so I told my tale to Mr. Tyler. Because of your delay, I raced over to Miss Susanna here and convinced her to still meet with you."

"Go on," Jane encouraged, "I recall, I dismissed you so I could to speak with Eliza Lucas."

Still catching her breath, Silversmith continued, "After you dismissed me, Mr. Tyler saw me in the dining area of the inn. The innkeeper has been so kind to both Billy and me that I sometimes help clear the breakfast tables when I can."

Jane nodded, "Very wise of you to ingratiate yourself as you did not know when I would arrive to settle your bill."

"Let the girl speak," Susanna Wright waved Jane to be silent. Silversmith looked at Jane for a signal and Jane nodded.

Silversmith said, "Mr. Tyler saw me there. I shared with him what I overheard. I reminded him that you asked me to meet you at the coffee house, so when he found Mr. Mossop, the opera singer, I went on to wait for you out in front of this place of coffee. We found Mr. Mossop at the docks when Mr. Tyler was confirming my story by making inquiries."

"But," Jane asked, "You were chasing Mr. Tyler and he is on horseback."

Susanna Wright asked, "What do you mean you went to the docks?"

"Mr. Mossop," Silversmith explained, "was secured by Mr. Tyler when I left. But, when I saw he had escaped... I knew I had to help, else you would never fulfill your Uncle's mission and you would not be at peace and we could not go home..."

Jane asked, "Uncle Floyd? What has an opera singer to do with Uncle Floyd's mission to help free colonial slaves?"

Susanna Wright persisted, "I'd like to know more about the docks... one boat in particular..."

"Mr. Mossop was caught because he was away from all his men," Silversmith explained to Jane, ignoring Susanna Wright.

Silversmith said, "I think Mr. Mossop may have been the one who hired Indians to attack people like Miss Polly. I told Mr. Tyler that if Mr. Mossop remained in the colonies, he would have harmed you, Miss Jane... He would have left you alone had you remained with Lady Sarah Wilson, Mr. Mossop's partner, but I had sent you the note summoning you before I overheard Mr. Mossop's plans."

Susanna Wright asked, "Docks? What did you ask at the dock? No. I correct myself. What did you discover at the docks as a result of your Mr. Tyler's questioning?"

Silversmith replied, "Mr. Henry Mossop is in a great deal of debt. He hired other men to assist him, also in debt. He developed a plan with Lady Sarah Wilson to get money the fastest way possible."

"Fastest way?" Jane asked.

Silversmith replied, "Yes, Miss Jane. Through selling Colonists, such as Polly's husband."

Jane exclaimed, "What?"

Silversmith continued, "Miss Jane, Mr. Tyler is working with Magistrate Pinkney to resolve these issues. Mr. Tyler had Mr. Mossop secured, but it was only after I saw him gallop by that I saw Mr. Mossop escaped. I ran to provide aid, you see. I returned once I saw Mr. Tyler and that Magistrate had things well in hand. Mr. Mossop won't escape, now."

"That's why," Susanna Wright proclaimed, "Henry Mossop infiltrated the barn meetings! He was a spy, paid to sow seeds of doubt and discontent, and to decide whom he would kidnap next and sell."

Jane shook her head, "I'm not understanding..."

Susanna Wright replied, "I understand!" Susanna looked at Jane, "Do you recall when I told you I had another appointment after our meeting?"

"Yes?" Jane replied, "Moving something?"

"Indeed. I must move a person. If Henry Mossop was discovered, caught, escaped, then found again, I suspect he sought restitution on the man I was trying to keep safe until a very important meeting. I must see if the man I was charged to guard is still safe. Would you excuse me, ladies?"

Jane asked, "Might we provide some assistance to you?"

"Ah," Susanna paused before replying, "I welcome your aid, but I must warn you my matter requires the utmost discretion. Both of you must promise me that you will never breathe a word of my plan to… anybody…" she warned with an examining look, "Ever."

Both Jane and Silversmith looked at each other uncertain as to how to respond.

2 CHAPTER 103: (JULY 1 1776) Bryce Corners Henry Mossop

With firearm grasped in one hand and reins in the other, Bryce Aiden Tyler forced the fleeing opera singer turn slave trader, Henry Mossop, into the awaiting red coats of Magistrate Karl Pinkney's men.

Seeing Henry Mossop race by the coffee house, where her mistress Jane was meeting with Susanna Wright, Silversmith took it upon herself to run to assist Bryce Aiden Tyler so that Henry Mossop could not escape. Once she saw Henry Mossop could not slip away from the red coated solders of the magistrate, Bryce gave her the nod and Silversmith raced back to the coffee house to rendezvous with Jane Hargreaves and Susanna Wright.

Bryce smiled as he saw Silversmith scamper away. She was a diligent worker and her efforts may very well help right a wrong. Bryce wondered if she realized how helpful she actually was.

While still keeping his eye on Henry Mossop, Bryce Aiden Tyler slowed his horse down to a walk. Hooves struck against the cobble stones with each disciplined step. The steed proved to be an imposing figure backing Henry Mossop into the awaiting muskets of the Magistrate's uniformed men.

"Please," Henry Mossop begged as he saw the red coat's expressionless faces, "I'm on your side. I work for your King. All my actions are not only legal, they are heroic and patriotic."

Magistrate Karl Pinkney stepped forward and spoke slowly, "Did nobody inform you, Mr. Mossop?"

The red-coated men gripped Henry Mossop firmly as the Magistrate completed his thought, "In this land we are establishing consistent rules across all colonies, so you cannot simply pick and choose which laws to violate. There will be consequences, you see. If, by some chance, there might be some exalted official in his Majesty's courts who has rewarded you for past behavior... perhaps we should have a detailed discussion about that..."

On the magistrate's signal, his men marched Henry Mossop inside a building, one oft times used as the local jail.

Satisfied, Bryce Aiden Tyler slipped off his horse, tethered it, gave his steed a loving pat and then strode inside the same building, following after Magistrate Karl Pinkney and his men.

3 CHAPTER 104: (JULY 2 1776)
Heading to the docks to find him

Silversmith had explained why Mr. Tyler was chasing the Irish opera singer and friend of Lady Sarah Wilson. Jane Hargreaves, Silversmith's mistress, was still perplexed, but offered her assistance, nonetheless, to her newly found friend Susanna Wright. Jane trusted Susanna because she heard so many nice stories about Susanna from her travelling companion, Eliza Lucas, who was staying at the same Inn as Jane.

16

Just that morning, Jane had breakfast with Eliza Lucas, to learn more about her plans to grow commercial Indigo plants all over the Colonies. Eliza sought business advice from Susanna Wright, and had consulted Susanna several times before. Today was the first time Jane was to meet Susanna Wright and she wanted to learn all about Miss Wright from Miss Lucas.

During the time when Jane Hargreaves was consulting Eliza Lucas, Indigo cultivator, about Susanna Wright, Silversmith had assisted Bryce Aiden Tyler in finding, identifying, and corralling the Irish Opera Singer and partner of Lady Sarah Wilson, Mr. Henry Mossop.

Silversmith explained why she ran away from the coffee shop where Miss Jane and Susanna Wright were sipping coffee, as she had to help chase Mr. Mossop into the arms of the Magistrate's men.

Once Susanna Wright heard Silversmith's story, Susanna Wright became quite agitated as if a well- hidden plan of hers had become undone.

Jane and Silversmith offered their assistance to Susanna Wright and promised to keep anything they were exposed to a secret.

Susanna Wright led Jane and Silversmith to a storage hut.

Jane Hargreaves was not expecting to see Eliza Lucas, let alone witness Susanna Wright rush over to Eliza Lucas, who was now half way inside the storage hut door. It was as if both women had agreed to meet here and they were late for something. Worry laced both the faces of Eliza Lucas and Susanna Wright.

Eliza Lucas was already inside this storage hut and was just emerging, stepping backwards onto the street from inside the hut. She looked relieved to see Susanna Wright rushing to her side with urgency.

Jane said, "Come along, Silversmith!" and gathered up her skirts to quicken her pace and catch up to Susanna Wright, "We must keep up with those two."

Without a word, all four women, Eliza Lucas, Jane Hargreaves, Susanna Wright and Silversmith looked inside the storage hut.

"Is this where you keep your indigo dyes?" Jane asked, breaking the silence, noting various clutter on the shelves and a blanket on the floor.

"Well, where is he?" Susanna asked Eliza.

"There is his food, blankets... see?" Eliza pointed at the half eaten morsels. "He knew to stay here until somebody came for him. I don't think he decided to go for a walk."

"What are we looking for?" Jane asked, "A hound? A child? An adult?"

Susanna replied, "We need to find him! Silversmith said he may be at the docks."

Silversmith replied, "Who is at the docks? I only found Mr. Mossop and he is well under lock and key by now..."

Jane looked to Eliza, "What sort of business advice were you seeking from Susanna Wright, Eliza?"

Susanna Wright waved them away from the storage hut, "We must head to the docks. Just because that opera singing Mossop is accounted for..."

"You mean," Eliza asked Susanna Wright, "His men may still try to take him?" While quickening her pace, Susanna shot back, "Men and their pride."

Jane piped in, "Pride?"

Susanna explained, "If their plans are interrupted, even if they are plans involving a great injustice, they will try to duel or somehow defend their non-existent honor."

Jane replied, "But who is missing and who are we chasing? Silversmith, perhaps you should go fetch Mr. Tyler and the Magistrate."

Susanna Wright stopped and looked at Jane. "Mr. Mossop is finally caught. If you lure away your Mr. Tyler, Mr. Mossop will escape again and continue his business. The same business your Uncle wanted to stop."

Silversmith looked to Jane for direction. Jane replied, "Stay with us, Silversmith."

"Yes, Miss." Silversmith replied while keeping up the clip of the walk. They were heading to the docks. The scent of seaweed, salt air and fish drifted over them, confirming they were walking in the correct direction.

Jane looked to Eliza and asked, "Who is missing?"

"A fellow who showed up at some meetings Susanna attended," Eliza replied.

Susanna added, "He was a servant, but his eloquence of speech betrayed his education and he relayed a tale of capture and escape to us. Our meeting was raided and I got him to safety. Without proof, I suspected Mr. Mossop had hired natives to kidnap others like him. We needed to keep this fellow safe as he is the only one who escaped and made his way to us. We wanted to craft a message to His Majesty with a real person to show proof of the abuses Colonists suffer."

"Why," Jane mentioned as she picked up her skirts with both hands and started to judiciously gasp for air between her words as she kept up with the other ladies.

Jane asked Susanna, "That is the exact same mission my uncle was working on... Is that how you were able to convey my mission so accurately at the coffee house?"

Susanna simply said, "Yes."

Eliza Lucas added, "It is something we are all aware of and have tried to stop for a very long time. Somehow those who oppose His Majesty's rule are intimidated and suddenly disappear, jailed for no particular reason, or become slaves. Button was the first one who had escaped it all..."

"Button?" Jane stopped.

Silversmith added, "Is that a common name to give at birth around here? For a man?"

Jane quickened her pace and with a look, both Silversmith and Jane knew they had to find out more about who this Button fellow was. Could it be Polly's missing husband? Or was it just a coincidence?

Susanna Wright urged, "We've no time to discuss baby names, Ladies. Come."

The ding of brass bells on a ship rang out. Men lugging cargo in nondescript sacs were gruffly going about their business.

Eliza asked Susanna Wright, "Did the documents arrive? The ones to be signed?" The ships and boats were gently bobbing up and down in the salty waters.

"They cannot all," Susanna replied to Eliza, "sign it on the same day. We may need to arrange for secret delivery and have it signed over a period of time."

Eliza replied, "Did they make copies?"

Susanna replied, "They were to arrive at the Inn by carriage last night, July first. I have not had time to see if they have arrived. You are at the Inn... did you notice if they arrived?"

Shaking her head Eliza reminded Susanna, "It is already the second day of July!" Eliza warned, "He must be at that meeting and the documents must be at the meeting, as well."

Looming before them were ships readying for departure.

"I cannot be at two places at once. We best find him before any of these vessels leave..." Susanna proclaimed, "And assume whoever delivered the documents will know where to deliver them."

4 CHAPTER 105: (JULY 2 1776)
Kidnapped, again!

Suddenly finding himself encased in burlap cloth, Button awoke to find he had to rely on his other senses as his vision was obscured.

With light leaking in between the woven fibers, Button concluded it must be early evening by now with the strong sun still beaming, but near setting. He could feel moist air and the smells of seaweed and fish gave him enough clues to alert him to his location. He was approaching a sailing vessel at the docks.

He could hear the repeated dings of a bell echoing over the sound of gently lapping waves hitting the sides of wooden hulls. Men shouting in the distance as they coordinated efforts to unfurl sails and then the sudden WHOMP WHOMP of the cloth being fully raised and filling with the salty air.

The sound of lapping water reminded Button of his voyage over to these Colonies. It was a rough voyage where the only good thing was meeting his wife, Polly, who may very well be dead...

These mixed emotions, evoked by the sound of lapping waves, made Button even more determined to avoid any travel by boat at any cost. If he were being brought onto a boat in a burlap bag, then his only conclusion was that he would be sold in some other land as a slave, assuming he would survive the voyage over.

Button felt himself being bumped along on some sort of cart. Now he was dumped out onto the ground and dragged with a grunt up a wooden incline. Button concluded that he must have awoken ahead of when his captor, a man who was panting for breath and obviously not physically of his prime, had expected. He noticed his mouth was stuffed with dirty cloth, which muffled any sounds he tried to make.

He decided he best not make any noise at all so he would not put his captor on guard. Button realized he had to plan another escape. This time, he had not been captured by Indians, but by those who hired the Indians. They were determined to ship a full boat of slaves and his escape had especially offended their honor.

Button was not surprised they sought him out, found him in that storage hut where Susanna Wright had stashed him. Knocked him over the head and took him to make money at the next slave market.

Roughly, he was pushed and shoved as if he were luggage. He was not.

Then, through the weave of the fabric, Button noticed the sun was fading. The air was getting cooler. He could see some men were lighting lanterns and candles. Tiny spots of light would appear over here and then there.

Who would set sail at night when there was limited visibility? Button was no sailor, but he assumed sailors who depart from port under the cloak of darkness either were enacting a mission of great urgency or one of foul depravity, such as stealthy theft.

Button concluded this is was the latter, a deed most foul. Button hoped he could have until morning to attempt an escape, but he wondered what if they locked him in iron shackles? Then, he really would be helpless to return to land.

No, he had to figure a way to never board this vessel.

Struggle as he did; strain as he might; his bonds would not budge. His mouth, dried by the fabric gag, still had a working tongue and he used that to push the gag out of his mouth. Then, he rubbed his face against his shoulder and was able to lower a corner of the gag.

Now he lay alone. As if whoever dumped him at the base of this ramp had gone to either take a break or get assistance. Button knew he would require more than one man to move him.

As he heard footsteps walk by, he tried to call out, but the only reaction he got was an occasional halting of walking, a humph uttered from a pedestrian as they thought they heard something and then resumed. There was too much noise at the docks to be understood and Button was disguised as just one sac piled among many. Passing footsteps stopped, he heard the soles of the boots pivot and pause and then continue on, leaving Button encased like a sausage in a scratchy potato sac.

It was not yet over.

The pace of the footsteps running away, appeared to run to some sort of supervisor to get advice or assistance because now Button heard two sets of boots quickly running toward him.

Then an odd thing happened.

Button overheard one man saying something and the voice sounded familiar... He thought and thought... where had he heard that man's voice?

Ah, it came to him.

It was a man to whom he had served water at the secret barn meetings.

He was not at the previous meetings but he was at this last Barn meeting, the one which was raided forcing Susanna Wright to pull Button down a hidden tunnel to escape.

This man boldly wore a red velvet coat at the meetings and Button found that odd that this man would mimic the King's red coated uniforms at a meeting where the topic was how to halt the abuses of the King.

Button thought hard... who was this man with... Why did he remember this voice?

Ah yes. Button now recalled in his thoughts that this man was always at the side of the opera singer, Henry Mossop, who was so outspoken.

Henry Mossop had given Button a punch in the stomach before he stomped out of the barn infuriated. This red velvet coated assistant was by his side the entire time.

Sometimes it is the quiet ones who give deference to their boisterous employer's rants and ravings that one must be careful of.

Yes. It was the man at the barn meeting who must have found him, as Susanna Wright had warned Button.

Button heard the footsteps of expensive leather boots approach, then click open what must have been a pocket watch as Button heard the light yet rapid hummingbird like ticking.

Impatiently, the device was snapped shut once more. Button concluded that time must be running out for the owner of the pocket watch. Or perhaps this man was waiting for somebody who hadn't shown up at a pre-determined time.

Then the man standing lowered his mouth to the prone burlap sack in which Button was encased. Button could feel his hot moist breath misting through the burlap weave.

The man and said, "I do not know if you are awake or not, but if you can hear me, know this... You will be boarded on that ship. You will refer to me as Mr. Tweedbottom, your master. You will do everything I instruct, else you will be tossed overboard to your death... Do you understand me, Slave?"

Button decided to remain motionless, so as to give the impression of still being unconscious, but his eyes were wide open.

Ah, yes. Where was the distinctive voice of the opera singer, Henry Mossop? Button listened, but heard nothing.

This man, which Button was now introduced to as a Mr. Tweedbottom, was waiting for his employer, Button assumed.

What would this Mr. Tweedbottom do to Button should the man who obviously paid him, that obnoxious Mr. Mossop, never show up?

5 CHAPTER 106: (JULY 2, 1776) Button and The Good Samaritan

"You there!" a helpful sailor called out to Mr. Tweedbottom as the light was fading at the dock.

The sailor lowered the sac he was carrying over one shoulder, resting it a few feet away from where Mr. Tweedbottom stood.

The sailor heartily approached Mr. Tweedbottom saying, "Our ship just

35

docked. Can you tell me where is the nearest inn? In payment, I can help you heave that luggage up the ramp, sir. I've little money as we've been at sea..."

"No. Assistance is quite un-necessary. Not necessary at all. I can manage," Tweedbottom explained as the sturdy well- muscled sailor evaluated the soft features of Mr. Tweedbottom, "I implore you to be about your business, Sailor."

The sailor shrugged, "Since we are new in this port, I just wanted to know where the Inn was before the weather turns..." he started to head back to his sac and was about to bend down to pick it up.

"Just arrived, eh?" Tweedbottom asked as he stepped over the burlap sack, which held Button and engaged the sailor in conversation, "Where was your last port of call?"

Mr. Tweedbottom realized that perhaps this sailor had seen Henry Mossop, the opera singer who was supposed to have met Mr. Tweedbottom and the other fellow in Mr. Mossop's employ. Mr.Tweedbottom had just suggested the other fellow race off to find where Mr. Mossop had gone and why he was late as they did need to set sail.

"Our last port was Ireland," the sailor smiled, "Can I exchange my muscle for your information or did you just arrive?" The sailor pointed to the motionless burlap sack, which lay behind Mr. Tweedbottom.

"No, no..." Mr. Tweedbottom smiled, "I'll manage," He paused and pointed in the direction of town and added, "The inn is in the center of town. That way."

The sailor smiled, nodded, and then turned in the direction Mr. Tweedbottom indicated. "Um," Mr. Tweedbottom said.

"Yes?" The sailor turned back around to face Mr. Tweedbottom. His eyes fell on the burlap sack behind Mr. Tweedbottom and the sailor squinted his eyes. Did the sac just move? Or was it his imagination.

Well, he was new here and may be in town for a spell, so didn't want to upset the locals. The sailor resumed eye contact with Mr. Tweedbottom.

"Ireland?" Mr. Tweedbottom asked.

The sailor paused, as if he heard something... a grunt perhaps? But, he was tired, so he dismissed the notion and continued to answer Mr. Tweedbottom.

"Just pulled into port." The sailor responded.

"And," Tweedbottom hesitantly asked, "Is anybody there awaiting passage back to Ireland?"

The sailor cocked his head to the side as he thought he heard a muffled grunt, but could not tell from whence it came as the sound seemed to come from the ground. Briefly, the sailor looked around and then reasoned he had heard the noises of this new place because he was so tired after such a long journey.

"We mostly transport cargo, sir," The sailor explained, "Any passenger may find it... uncomfortable. I don't think there will be a ship heading to Ireland for some time, yet. But, you'd have to ask the captain about that... He's over..."

The rays of the sun were starting to slip back, retreating over the horizon and revealing the stars, which would soon be a sharp contrast to an inky sky. The sailor looked up. His expression betrayed that he read the weather better than Mr. Tweedbottom. The sailor shook his head as if to confirm in his own mind that he would need the shelter of an inn to avoid any foreboding winds.

He walked back over to the sac, which he dropped earlier a few feet away and extracted a small lantern.

Mr. Tweedbottom waved away the notion and said, "No need to trouble your captain, Sailor... So, no... uh... gentleman... greeted you when you docked and requested passage back to Ireland," Mr. Tweedbottom confirmed.

"I'm looking for an inn to lay my head," the sailor replied, "We, who did travel, are exhausted and I'd like to tell them where we can sleep tonight."

The sailor lit the lantern, closing the door of the unit to allow the flame to be shielded from puffs of wind originating from the waters. He set the lantern on the ground allowing the glow to illuminate his sac as he tied it shut, once more. The sailor picked up his sac and threw it over one shoulder, then bent his knees until he could pick up the top of the lantern with his free hand.

He turned back to see if Mr. Tweedbottom needed anything else.

"Quite," Mr. Tweedbottom sympathized, "That way." He pointed again in the direction of town.

Mr. Tweedbottom smiled. If Henry Mossop had not shown up to this ship, nor had he sought passage back to Ireland, then...

"If the other fellow," Mr. Tweedbottom said to himself, "Ran away once he discovered that Henry Mossop had missed our appointment and he is not back by now... and if Henry Mossop is not seeking to flee on a vessel from Ireland.... Then if I leave now, I won't need to share the profits with either of them and I'll have enough to start my own slave venture..."

Mr. Tweedbottom watched as the sailor's lantern swung effortlessly over to a group of people. This small gathering was presumably from the same ship. Mr. Tweedbottom observed them from a distance and noted that this sailor pointed in the same direction, which Tweedbottom had indicated the direction of the Inn.

The others picked up various sacs or cases and slowly stumbled on their way.

6 CHAPTER 107: (JULY 2 1776) Primo Uomo Defense

"You have no right to bring me here, I am in the employ of the British Empire. I work for your king," the opera singer boomed to the red-coated soldiers, as he stomped around the tiny room in which he was secured.

With the magistrate having had selected which men would be stationed at each town, he was fortunate to have the luxury of travelling only with his red-coated driver, and then have willing trained men at each location to do the Magistrate's bidding.

In this case, the soldiers in Meeting Town had been instructed to have flat expressions and to never speak to Mr. Mossop even if he attempted to provoke conversation while in this cramped tiny room. It was a tactic the Magistrate had heard about from an Italian friend who shared this as a successful pre-interrogation technique used by Venetian Doges.

Once Magistrate Karl Pinkney and Bryce Aiden Tyler entered the room, the magistrate's men silently and methodically marched out and stood in front of the door to guard against any attempted escape.

Magistrate Pinkney started. "I believe you are in debt, Mr. Mossop. Your lavish lifestyle exceeds the money you have made from your performances in Europe and you came to this land to try a new profession."

"How could you possibly know that?" the opera singer gasped, "Did that woman..."

Bryce Aiden Tyler suggested, "Why do you think your confidences would be betrayed by one charlatan. Surely there are others with whom you have done business who could be easily swayed by the Magistrate's influence...no?"

The suggestion caused Henry Mossop's thoughts to race and suspect every person he had ever engaged with.

"I have other sources of income, sir..." The opera singer protested.

Magistrate Pinkney calmly explained, "We have witnesses which will swear in court that you have..."

"She betrayed me!" Henry Mossop slammed his fist into the wall infuriated.

"Who, Mr. Mossop?" Bryce Aiden Tyler asked.

Henry Mossop puffed, "Marchioness de Waldegrave, sister to the Queen herself..." He rubbed his eyes and then said, "Maybe it was that tailor...."

"Do you, by chance mean," Bryce tried to recall all the details Silversmith had shared with him earlier, "by Marchioness de Waldegrave, sister to the Queen... a woman known as Lady Sarah Wilson?"

"Or," Henry Mossop declared, "Any of her other aliases."

Magistrate Pinkney said calmly, "There was a woman who had worked for Her Majesty and had stolen dresses and jewels from Queen Charlotte around 1771. I suspect this Lady Sarah Wilson is that person. I do not believe she is the queen's actual sister."

"Of course not, but she betrayed me nonetheless!" Henry Mossop fumed as he looked at the Magistrate and pleaded, "Tell me who it was, please..."

Bryce, as the Magistrate and Bryce had

rehearsed earlier, interrupted with, "Magistrate Pinkney, I do not think you need to tell Mr. Mossop of every person who has betrayed him..."

Bryce got all his information from Silversmith and he knew the word of a maid against the reputation of a famous singer would not bode well in court. He had to be clever and trick Henry Mossop into revealing his plan.

The Magistrate picked up the cue and said to Bryce, "Agreed. Perhaps it is better if we hear the details from Mr. Mossop as there is a chance he has been falsely accused. I'm sure he is aware that we shall be scheduling a suitable form of execution for Mr. Mossop. Those who gave us information will remain free as they provided helpful incriminating evidence against Mr. Mossop. "

Again, as the Magistrate and Bryce Aiden Tyler had discussed before Henry Mossop was captured, Magistrate Karl Pinkney extracted a formal letter from his jacket only half written. Bryce went to the side of the room and found a quill and inkwell, bringing both objects over to the Magistrate, with an obsequious bow.

Henry Mossop fervently nodded his head, "I was not the leader, the tailor was. It is he who should be executed." With a confused expression, Henry Mossop looked at the parchment in the Magistrate's hands.

"Indeed?" the Magistrate nodded calmly as he waved his wrist in a rolling motion to encourage Mr. Mossop to continue, "And who is paying for your decisions about who should die and who should be kidnapped?"

It was not yet time to inform Henry Mossop about the nature of this half written letter.

"Oh," Henry Mossop smiled, "We only have killed those who would interfere with the plans of the Crown... just as you do, Mr. Magistrate."

"I see," The Magistrate nodded, "the cost of doing business?"

"Yes!" Henry Mossop enthusiastically agreed, hopeful that now the Magistrate was sympathetic to him and would soon release Henry Mossop due to this misunderstanding. Henry Mossop even looked at his pocket watch as he noted the time.

"Are we keeping you from an appointment, Mr. Mossop?" Bryce Aiden Tyler asked.

"Oh," Mr. Mossop took a step toward the door, "I'm so glad you understand. I do have a meeting. Could I enlist your assistance in securing a carriage to take me to the docks?"

Bryce Aiden Tyler stepped between Henry Mossop's egress and the door, preventing him from even touching the handle of the door.

"Do sit," the Magistrate politely offered as he indicated a chair.

Slowly, Henry Mossop walked back to the other chair by the small table and sat as Bryce Aiden Tyler remained standing, looking down at him.

"You see," Magistrate Pinkney explained, "I must apologize for the manner in which we brought you here. We understand you have a full schedule. I also have other matters to attend to, so perhaps you could simply enlighten me about a subject which confuses me and then we can resume our activities." He smiled.

"Oh, of course. I am in full support of the King's business." Henry Mossop exclaimed, "Let me resolve your questions and I'll be on my way."

"Splendid," Magistrate Pinkney smiled as he clasped his hands, "Again, I apologize for the rough handling by which my men secured you, but there was no other way we could get your attention. I really have no interest in setting up an execution... All I wanted to do was write a letter to the Crown praising your deeds in support of the Crown. Such letters are best written with examples so that we can show that you have cooperated with me and my men all along. This is why it is imperative I have details so I may boast about your successes with accuracy, should a more senior official question me. First, I must ask, do you have formal papers issued by His Majesty detailing the enterprise in which you are engaged?"

"Oh, well actually no. You see the details of my engagement were made by a member of his Courts. Because it was a secret, I have no papers," Henry Mossop apologized.

"I see," The Magistrate understood, "then perhaps you could furnish me with the details and I could write a letter of gratitude to His Majesty for your utmost bravery. I'm sure there would be a reward for all your efforts, but I would require details... You understand?"

"Oh, naturally," Henry Mossop agreed, "I would very much enjoy pleasing even more gold out of the King's treasury."

The Magistrate continued, "Then, do elaborate with examples of those you have dispensed with."

"Well, there were so many," Henry Mossop explained, "But I was careful as to use the natives to execute the tasks so you, Your Magistrate, would never be sullied by the deeds."

"And I am rather grateful to you, My good man," Magistrate Karl Pinkney affirmed, "Simply summarize it for me..."

"Very well," Henry Mossop took a breath, "Several have tried to halt our enterprise, but I have made an agreement with a Lady Sarah Wilson, who has been able to find names of gentlemen who oppose our cleansing efforts."

Bryce asked, "By 'cleansing' do you mean ridding our area of those who wish to frustrate the King's plans to rule these lands?"

"Exactly," Henry Mossop explained, "As a matter of fact, there was one fellow, a man of business. He actually tried to organize some to follow the Indians we hired and stop their attempts to secure inventory."

"And by 'inventory'", Bryce Aiden Tyler asked, "do you mean the colonists who object to the rule of His Majesty?"

The Magistrate leaned forward and asked, "And how did you rid yourself of this annoying business fellow."

"Yes. Yes. Yes," Henry Mossop nodded, "Well, we ignored him at first, but he actually undid plans for several of our raids and that cost us quite a bit. We are a small business venture, you see, and cannot compete with those larger ships, which go to foreign lands to get slaves. Our niche is to simply rid the colonies of disloyal souls and profit from it."

"Ingenious," Bryce prodded, "So how did you rid yourself of this man?"

Inhaling deeply, Henry Mossop continued, "Well, I heard that one Indian fellow had met with this business man and alerted him to the fact that some tribe members were hired to take the tainted colonists from their homes. So, I hired another Indian to meet with the man of business and simply leave some supplies hidden in his study."

"To what end?" the Magistrate asked.

"Well, so that I could ask one of my men to later execute him and make it appear as self-murder. You see," Henry Mossop explained, "Being on stage has educated me about techniques used to make the audience think what you want them to."

"Do go on..." Magistrate Pinkney encouraged.

"Well," Henry Mossop continued, "One of my men is very creative. He concocted an idea which I felt was commendable."

"Yes?" Bryce asked.

53

Henry Mossop responded with, "He was able to shoot that fellow earlier in the day when nobody was in the house. He had befriended the other occupants of this man's household and made certain they were all distracted when the deed was done. Then, he took the elements planted by the Indian I hired…"

"Indian? A Tall fellow?" Bryce asked.

Mr. Mossop explained, "Oh, I don't recall how tall he was, but this business fellow had met with that one other Indian fellow so I knew nobody would suspect that another Indian would visit him. Nobody realized the true purpose was to leave supplies for my hireling."

"Go on," The Magistrate prodded.

"In sum," Henry Mossop smiled as he rose from his chair and glanced at the door, "my man shot him in his own home. Nobody heard it. Later, he set it up to obliterate any footprints left on the floor. He also managed to set off a delayed bang to provide him with the cover of innocence. The deed was thereby done and everybody still thinks it was self-murder or that of some spirit because there were no footprints."

"Were there no... loose threads? No witnesses?" the Magistrate asked.

Henry Mossop replied, "Well, the fellow had a young relative. A niece. She started to become curious, so I have arranged to rid myself of her, just as a precautionary measure."

"And this clever hireling of yours..." Bryce Aiden Tyler asked, "Would that be a Mr. Tweedbottom?"

"Yes!" Henry Mossop exclaimed, "You see. He was helping his Majesty. There is a promise of great wealth offered by an official in His Majesty's Treasury. This official has been very successful with obtaining the estates of colonists over here by simply accusing them of crimes, you see. Nobody ever investigates charges issued from England, so he also suggested our enterprise. Rather brilliant, you see."

"Really?" The magistrate said as he straighten up and tilted his head, "Do tell me how that scheme works."

Henry Mossop felt that His Majesty would not risk upsetting the monarchs of other lands who have also sent subjects to this great immense island, the British Americas, so had hired Mossop and his men to exact a very valuable service. Rid the colonies of individuals who do not actively support the British Crown.

"Simple, really," Henry Mossop shrugged, "He gets names of people who have left for the colonies. He has people here who verify those selected have property here in the colonies. Then, he writes up the paperwork and hands the names of the accused to be officially signed. You see, with all the battles and wars, His Majesty doesn't have time to look at each piece of paper, let alone verify if it is valid. The sentence is always to liquidate assets and return the funds to the courts. It is those funds which support my enterprise, thereby not impacting His Majesty's books at all."

"So, these Colonists with property," Magistrate Karl Pinkney clarified, "Do not need to have actually committed a crime. They simply need to own something of value, which can be sold to be sent back to England and then fund... you... Is that correct? I only wish I knew about this earlier..."

"Exactly. Everybody wins." Henry Mossop continued, "An artist requires a patron!"

The Magistrate interjected, "I only wish I knew of these happenings to the Colonists my men were instructed to keep safe by enforcing order... You see His Majesty, King George, has charged me to keep order in my jurisdiction and I had no idea of your enterprise."

Henry Mossop scrambled with, "If you, Mr. Magistrate, find the permanent removal of treasonous souls in your jurisdiction somehow objectionable, then I would like to remind you that I did not actually execute any snuffing out of any colonist. It was Mr. Tweedbottom who planned and executed all the colonist murders. I only orchestrated the kidnappings for sale at the slave market."

Bryce asked Henry Mossop, "And could you kindly provide the name of this interfering business man who frustrated your plans? For the letter which Magistrate Pinkney will write on your behalf..."

"Oh, right. Details," Henry Mossop said, "Floyd Hargreaves. Well, he was the last one. I have other names If you feel that would help my achievements more noticeable to His Majesty. I'm already looking forward to a great reward, you see, and welcome even more gold...Will you kindly summon a carriage for me, now?"

7 CHAPTER 108: (JULY 2 1776) The women and the Irish Sailor

As Susanna Wright, Eliza Lucas, Jane Hargreaves and her maid, Silversmith approached the docs, they came across a group of weary travelers who appeared to be heading into town, just as they were emerging from it.

One man with a sac over his shoulder, walked in front with a lantern swinging in front of him. Susanna Wright approached him with "Pardon us, Sir, but may we ask you a question?"

The sailor replied, "We are on our way to the town Inn after a long voyage."

Jane Hargreaves evaluated the group, huddled together to shield each other from the dropping temperature. The sailor with the lantern handed the lantern to one of them and waved them on their way as he remained with the four ladies, Susanna, Jane, Eliza and Silversmith.

Susanna Wright without acknowledging the others had continued on, replied, "Have you seen a man. Not a sailor, but..."

"You mean," The sailor replied, "Like a gent in a red velvet coat? No sailor could afford to wear that."

"Red velvet?" Jane asked as she looked at Silversmith.

The sailor lazily pointed behind him and said, "He asked me if we were returning to Ireland soon and if a gent asked for passage."

"Ireland!" Silversmith exclaimed.

"Yes, Ireland. Just arrived. Pleasant evening, ladies." The sailor stated as he quickened his pace to join his companions. As he left, the ladies overheard the sailor's voice fading, "why is everybody in this port so curious about how to get to Ireland?"

Silversmith turned to Jane with, "Miss Jane. If Mr. Tyler has that opera singer Henry Mossop secured, perhaps the original plan was that he set sail back to his home in Ireland."

Jane replied, "And I know that my friend Mr. Tweedbottom enjoys wearing a red velvet coat. Could it be that he and Henry Mossop worked together to take Button?"

"Henry Mossop," Silversmith added, "Knew Lady Sarah Wilson better than you did and we know Mr. Tweedbottom was in his shadow while you stayed at the estate..."

"I just find it so difficult to believe, Silversmith." Jane mused.

"With Henry Mossop stopped," Susanna Wright urged, "We must assume that Button is being held captive by your Mr. Tweedbottom. Come. Let us find the vessel on which he plans to sail."

"Surely," Eliza Lucas asked, "Mr. Tweedbottom would not leave without Mr. Mossop and Mr. Mossop is in the hands of the Magistrate's men."

Silversmith shook her head, "Perhaps Mr. Tweedbottom wanted to determine if Mr. Mossop was seeking passage to Ireland. Is that not from whence that sailor's ship had just come? Is Ireland not the home of Mr. Henry Mossop? Perhaps if Mr. Tweedbottom does have Button as a captive, it is possible there are other slaves on the same ship..."

"Then, we must hurry..." Jane quickened her pace behind Susanna Wright.

8 CHAPTER 109: (JULY 2, 2015) The Women and Spot the Figure

The women had rounded a large building, obscuring one portion of the docks when they heard the cold wind whistle.

"Nobody would risk sailing on a night like tonight," Eliza Lucas commented as she wrapped her shawl around her, "Look at the docks, they are nearly deserted, now."

Jane suggested, "Perhaps a man unaccustomed with sailing, yet with the notion that he can do anything, would be foolish enough to attempt it. I just cannot believe that the man who said he was so devoted to me would... would... be involved in the enslavement of Colonists."

"One must take time to know a man's heart as it will betray his true character," Silversmith added. "If I may, Miss Jane, good that you did not tempt yourself with the possibility of becoming Mr.Tweedbottom's wife."

"Silversmith!" Jane admonished, "Let us see if we can find Button and then we can ascertain how to locate Polly to see if it is the Button she calls her husband."

"Look!" Eliza Lucas pointed.

Fog was settling in and images were difficult to discern. There was a man who looked as if he were dragging something up a ramp.

"That fellow is struggling," Susanna Wright commented, "He's not as thin as some of the other sailors."

"Look!" Eliza persisted with a whisper, "The clouds parted and the moon is shining on his jacket. It's red."

"Some of His Majesty's officers wear red coats…" Jane mentioned. "Is that not why some of the locals refer to them as 'red coats' or 'lobster backs'?"

"Ah," Susanna Wright retorted, "But the British Army would also wear white britches and a black hat. The navy may have blue coats… I think that fellow there is not military. I cannot see his britches, which means they must be black or some other dark color not of the King's uniform… and that fellow must be a civilian. Let us investigate if he is your Mr. Tweedbottom."

Silversmith asked, "What is in that sac he is dragging? Clearly too heavy. He's having to rest every few steps."

Jane uttered, "Not Polly's Button... it couldn't be..."

9 CHAPTER 110: (JULY 2, 2015) the Sailor Returns

In a shaft of moonlight peeking through the accumulating brooding clouds, a man in a red velvet jacket was seen laboring under the weight of dragging something up a ramp leading to the deck of a ship. The four women, Susanna Wright, Eliza Lucas, Jane Hargreaves and her maid, Silversmith, all witnessed it and collectively decided to investigate.

Clustered together, the four women pushed their skirts aside to form an imposing silhouette. They approached as silently as they could, realizing they must be a spectacle as their demeanor betrayed their trepidation with this unformed plan.

Susanna Wright turned around suddenly as she heard a noise behind her. It appeared as if somebody called out to the women.

Susanna whispered, "You go on, ahead. Let me investigate that shouting. If that voice is hailing us, it could be a dock guard on patrol. Let me see if he can render assistance, should we need it."

The three remaining women didn't have time to respond as Susanna Wright took a quick step backwards, pivoted, and then hurried to where she heard the sound.

Jane Hargreaves leaned over to Silversmith, "Keep an eye on her. Susanna Wright's protective bravery may lead her into a trap. It may not be a dock guard. We don't even know if we are hunting the right ship. Button could be in the center of town for all we know. If Susanna needs our assistance, Silversmith, yell or come fetch us..."

Silversmith nodded and quietly followed Susanna Wright. Susanna approached a swinging lantern.

"Ahoy, Lady. You, there..." the man's voice called.

Eliza Lucas turned to Jane Hargreaves, "Should we have also gone with Susanna and Silversmith? Should we not have all stayed together?"

"We are fine," Jane replied with confidence, "Susanna, I've noticed, is... bold... and that may get her into danger. Besides, as two women, we do not threaten anybody."

"You mean we are not commanding enough?" Eliza asked, "I can be forceful. I've had to manage three estates when my father is in the command of George Washington. I can be a mighty force."

"Eliza," Jane replied in soothing tones, "If it is my friend Mr. Tweedbottom, he simply needs to be spoken with in calm tones. He is a reasonable man. We enjoy taking tea together."

"And what if it is not Mr. Tweedbottom?" Eliza challenged, "We must show that one must fear women of purpose."

"Oh, Eliza," Jane shook her head," I don't think that is wise, either."

"If the sac is cargo, we apologize, but if it is a man..." Eliza suggested, "More force is in order."

"Then," Jane acquiesced, "Let us move slowly, but keep an eye on the man on the ship, but also an eye on Susanna, as Silversmith will retrieve her. That way, we shall be four ladies, not two."

Eliza Lucas and Jane Hargreaves leaned closer together as they linked arms, and slowly continued their approach toward the ship. Eliza glanced back to spy the light of the lantern.

"Ahoy there, Lady," The voice behind Jane and Eliza boomed.

Then, both Jane and Eliza assumed that Susanna must have reached the hailer, as now the tones of a man and a woman were more conversational and indiscernible.

The shout, however, alerted the shadowy velvet coated figure on the ship. He suddenly stood up, facing away from Jane and Eliza. He was nearly half way up the ramp. The sac appeared to be flopping partially off the ramp, precariously hovering over the dank cold lapping waters below.

Eliza and Jane froze in an inky shadow as they witnessed the figure rub his back, then look around. They saw him look in the direction of the lantern off in the distance. He shrugged his shoulders and turned his attentions to the sac at his feet. He resumed his tugging on the end of the burlap sack.

Susanna Wright approached the man who had called out and then, in the light of the lantern he held, she recognized him as the sailor with whom she had spoken but moments earlier.

Susanna Wright approached him with hands on her hips, "Sir? Do you summon us? Were you and your companions not wending toward the inn?"

He was very apologetic as he replied, "Yes. But, by the insistence of one of my companions, we fear the inn may not have enough room to accommodate us all. Well, since the streets are deserted, probably because of the brooding skies, I came to ask you..."

Susanna interrupted speaking more to herself, "I had assumed you were calling out to us because you were patrolling the docks."

"Patrolling? No Madame." The sailor replied, "I just wanted to ask..."

Susanna shook her head and cut him off again, "It's Miss Wright. Not Madame..." Susanna glanced over her shoulder to ascertain the progress of her friends.

The sailor's expression twisted into a perplexed visage as he peered over Susanna's shoulder and observed Susanna's two friends clustered together, slowly inching toward the ship.

It was the same ship from which this sailor had earlier sought directions to the town Inn.

Then Silversmith approached, "Miss Susanna," She surprised Susanna Wright.

"Silversmith, what are you doing here. You should be protecting your mistress." Susanna admonished.

Silversmith replied, "Miss Jane sent me to protect you." Silversmith looked at the sailor and folded her arms as menacingly as she could as she continued, "They don't know if Button is on that ship or if we need to approach a different vessel. They need you, Miss Susanna."

Susanna said hurriedly, "I must return to my friends, Mr. Sailor, sir. "

"Begging your pardon, but," The sailor said stopping Susanna and Silversmith from returning to their friends, "If the Inn is full, some can continue on and seek shelter at a certain church. Can you tell me how I may locate this church?" The sailor held out a paper and his lantern to show Susanna.

"I would ask the innkeeper," Susanna brusquely advised, as she nervously turned back looking for her friends, Jane and Eliza.

Both Jane and Eliza had kept watch on the dot of light in the darkness caused by the sailor's lantern. They observed the outlines of both Silversmith and Susanna Wright now returning to their location, leaving the glow of light, which gently bathed them.

The sailor persisted, "Miss Wright, Not all Innkeepers are known to be... godly... Just as not all sailors are... drunks. Please. Won't you give us instruction so that we may all rest this night, be it in the Inn or in a church?"

Feeling guilty, Susanna and the sailor quickly exchanged information.

Satisfied, the sailor turned back toward his awaiting weary travelling companions.

Likewise, Silversmith and Susanna Wright returned to toward the water to meet up with Eliza and Jane.

Susanna and Silversmith were both startled to hear the voice of Eliza Lucas shouting an order toward the figure on the boat.

Susanna Wright quickened her pace as she muttered to Silversmith, "That little Eliza is such a firebrand. She may get us all killed."

Silversmith replied, "Is that a firearm Miss Eliza is holding?"

10 CHAPTER 111: (JULY 2, 1776)
Eliza Shouts Orders

"Drop what you hold, Sir!" Eliza Lucas demanded as she sprinted up the ramp of the boat brandishing a firearm.

"Eliza!" Jane called after her as she followed. Tweedbottom stood upright in shock.

"Jane?" He asked.

"Hello..." Jane replied to Mr. Tweedbottom with a smile and wave behind Eliza's outstretched arm grasping the firearm.

Jane scrambled up the ramp and whispered to Eliza, "Where did you get that thing?"

Eliza whispered back, "It's how I keep my slaves in order. Ironic I'm using gunpowder to save a man from slavery. Is that hypocritical or ironic?"

Jane whispered, "It's a bit rash, as we can simply speak reason with Mr. Tweedbottom. We don't want to aggravate him needlessly."

Then, as if Eliza had not heard a word Jane said, she shouted at Mr. Tweedbottom, who stood at the top of the ramp and ordered him to, "Open that sac."

"You mean, this sac?" Tweedbottom kicked the unconscious form of Button encased in burlap. His body rolled down the ramp, proving to be an imposing obstacle for both Jane and Eliza.

Unperturbed, and rather annoyed, Eliza hopped over the lump rolling down the ramp and chased Mr. Tweedbottom up onto the deck of the vessel.

Jane, not as athletic as Eliza, barely kept her balance as she saw the sac rolling off to the side of the ramp. It was not, after all, a ball which would maintain a straight line of descent. As it precariously edged over the side of the ramp, threatening to plunk into the dark waters below, Jane grasped one end of the sac. Summoning all her might, Jane was barely able to manage the weight of the man and she felt her shoes slipping against the well-worn mist covered planks of the ramp.

"Heavy..." was all Jane could muster saying.

All at once, Jane felt the familiar hand of her maid, Silversmith grip around Jane, pulling her back as Susanna Wright rushed around to try and pull the other end of the sac back onto the ramp. After much effort, the trio was successful.

Jane grunted, "Eliza's chased him up there."

The three ladies managed to pull the burlap sack and its precious contents back onto the ramp, situating it in such a manner as to more easily roll it down the ramp.

Susanna asked, "Is it your Mr. Tweedbottom?" Jane sadly nodded with, "Yes..."

Susanna opened the sac to reveal the beaten face of Button, blood already drying from an earlier attack, presumably the boots of Mr. Tweedbottom.

Horrified, Jane turned to Silversmith, "Silversmith, find and fetch Mr. Tyler and the Magistrate. I think we will need his assistance."

"Somebody must tend to Mr. Button's wounds else he may die..." Susanna determined as she looked at him, "But he is bound in... what sort of device is this? Are these wooden shackles?"

Jane leaned over asking as she observed, "How does one open that?"

Susanna replied, "Presumably with a key. I cannot untie... wood. I could if it were rope, but wood?"

"Silversmith," Jane ordered, "fetch them, now. Let them know, we need a doctor. Be swift!" Silversmith nodded, then ran down the ramp and dashed off into the darkness.

They heard Eliza yelp up on deck.

Susanna started to get up and run up the ramp.

"No," Jane held out a hand, "Tend to

Button's wounds, even if you must patch him with scraps torn from your own skirts." Jane added, "Should that fellow actually be Polly's husband, I could never face Polly and tell her I watched a man named Button die and have her always wonder if it was her husband."

Susanna replied, "Simply fetch Eliza. We have the Button I need for that meeting. Our business is concluded. If it is your Mr. Tweedbottom, let him be on his way."

Jane nodded, "I'll fetch Eliza. I'm sure Mr. Tweedbottom will understand..."

Jane turned and precariously stepped firmly up the tiny ramp, her skirts hovering over the water on each side of the ramp as she ascended.

Susanna descended the ramp once more, dragging Button to the stable dock. She looked around and noticed the loud noises had ceased. The dinging of bells had stopped.

Nobody was around.

Susanna called out, but her voice only echoed and in reply she heard the lapping of waves and a bit of commotion from atop the ship she had just left.

Near the base, there was a cart and Susanna was able to roll Button into it, as she sought to find him shelter and warmth. She tugged the cart to the closest dark deserted building, which still had a view of the ship she had just left.

Keeping an eye on the ramp, expecting to see Eliza and Jane descend any moment, Susanna raced around in search of some implement, which could help her tend to the wounds suffered by Button.

The smell of dead fish was overwhelming, but Susanna Wright forged through and found a slab, presumably one used to chop fish, which were freshly caught.

She looked at the cart below and the limp form of Button, still in his burlap sack, but now with face exposed to the fresh air.

Susanna then looked at the elevated slab and back at her own hands. She shook her head. She would never be able to get Button's body up onto that slab.

Susanna took a step and nearly slipped as she realized her foot squished the end of a fish tail. Looking down, she could make out that there were several fish tails strewn about the ground. Some appeared to be tails from cod, haddock and yellow-tail flounder.

In the weak moonlight, her eye spied sacs piled against the wall. Over there was a barrel. Patting the slab before her, she hoped to find a knife.

"But," Susanna said aloud, "Would a knife help me loosen those wooden shackles?" She bit her lip.

Susanna Wright was tasked with tending to Button's wounds, and she was determined to do so faithfully.

Exhaling in frustration, Susanna Wright was unable to find any sharp implement around the room. It was as if the fish monger had taken all his knives home with him.

Anxious, Susanna Wright bumped the toe of her shoe against the base of another barrel pushed back in the shadows. She felt the side of it and the wood was worn smooth as if it had been used and washed out and scrubbed down numerous times. Any alcohol it had once contained inside was now long gone and this barrel was used for another purpose. The lid of the barrel was off, yet it did not appear to contain liquid. She could not ascertain what its contents were.

Susanna leaned her ear closer to the barrel opening and kicked the wooden tub, then listened. She heard scratches against the wood. She still could not see the contents. Kicking her toe about the base of the barrel, she found a plank of wood which now fell down with a loud clatter.

Grabbing the small piece of wood, Susanna plunged it inside the barrel, deeper and deeper until she heard a "clap".

Out, she pulled the now weighted down wood. On the end dangled a lobster, hanging onto the end of corner of the wooden plank with its mighty claw.

This barrel, she reasoned, was left unlocked because lobster was the food for servants. As anybody knew, lobsters were so plentiful and bland, that only the serfs would consume it. It did not surprise Susanna to find the barrel left here unattended and opened. Nobody would steal it.

The crustacean clung with such force to the end of Susanna's stick, that by the time Susanna pulled the small plank all the way out of the barrel and moved it from the mouth of the barrel to the floor, the lobster had snapped the corner off and fell to the ground, dazed by the impact.

Its sluggish movements were no match for the speedy Susanna Wright. She stepped on its tail, and knelt down, wrapping the body of the crustacean in the plentiful fabric of the hem of her skirts. She left the lethal claw exposed.

Slowly, the claw opened and closed, grasping and snapping in the air.

She brought the lobster over to the unconscious Button and judiciously positioned the lobster so that the wooden shackles, which bound him, were situated such that they were within snapping distance of the serrated-edged crusher claw.

The lobster claw started to rhythmically open and close, stopping only when it felt the wood in its grasp. It squeezed with such force that the wood between Button's hands started to splinter and groan. Once it had snapped clean though, Susanna moved to the wooden shackles, which bound Button's ankles and repeated the procedure. Button, who was still unconscious, finally was free. Now, Susanna could tend to his wounds.

She took one step backward toward the barrel to replace the lobster with its other lobster friends when she heard a great noise from outside.

Still holding the lobster in the hem of her skirts, and leaving the unconscious Button inside the cart, Susanna Wright raced outside and gasped at what she saw, helpless to do anything about it.

The winds increased with angry fervor and the sea churned. It had started to rain.

11 CHAPTER 112: (JULY 2, 1776): Jane finds Eliza, Moments Before the Splash

Jane raced up the plank to inform Eliza Lucas that they should go. Jane confidentially felt if she explained matters to Mr. Tweedbottom, that he would understand that Button was possibly the husband of her new friends and they would be on their way.

When she got to the deck, she noticed that Mr. Tweedbottom had already pulled up anchor. Eliza was still pointing her fire arm at him. Mr. Tweedbottom had one arm fully outstretched holding his own firearm aimed at Eliza.

"Mr. Tweedbottom," Jane exclaimed, "I'm sure this is all a misunderstanding. My friend Miss Lucas and I shall be going, now, do pardon our interruption." She curtseyed and beckoned Eliza to join her.

Eliza started to inch her way toward Jane Hargreaves and Mr. Tweedbottom kept his aim on her the entire time.

"I think not!" Mr. Tweedbottom replied loudly so as to be heard over the winds. "I lost one for sale and have replaced him with two. I find this an adequate exchange. Ladies, I ask you to move over there. Unless you want to risk which of you shall be shot first, that is."

"Mr. Tweedbottom! Sir!," Jane exclaimed, "It is I, your tea-time friend. Remember?"

"It is too late, Jane," Mr. Tweedbottom shouted, "I'm in charge, now and I am determined to complete what was started!"

"I'm afraid I don't understand, Mr. Tweedbottom..." Jane shook her head. Eliza asked Jane, "Are we drifting?"

Jane Hargreaves heard the odd groan of wood scraping against wood.

She glanced at Eliza and they both looked in the direction of the ramp, which they had both just used to climb aboard the ship. It was the only mode of egress, which Jane had planned on to disembark from this sailing vessel. That ramp had now splashed into the water, spraying salty cold mist onto the docks below, as the ship now drifted out to sea.

Jane glanced over the edge of the railing and saw the outline of a solitary Susanna Wright holding something wrapped in the hem of her skirts.

The winds filled the ship's sails and started to move more rapidly, which further pushed the ship away from the docks.

"Mr. Tweedbottom," Jane now shouted with urgency, "I demand to be returned to shore." The rain was getting heavier.

Jane glanced to see who was navigating this vessel, but when she spied the helm, it appeared to have been jammed into position with a rope or wooden stick. It was as if Mr. Tweedbottom had set course without any person needing to man the helm.

Then a huge wave curled up like a rising phoenix and crashed against the side of the ship.

12 CHAPTER 113: (JULY 2 1776)
Polly's Settles in the Inn

Comfortably situated in the Meeting Town Inn, Mrs. Dunlap, exhausted from the long journey, closed the door behind her as she walked into the rented guest room in which Polly Mulhoolin was staying.

Mrs. Dunlap, the printer's wife, walked to Polly, who was in bed and plumped up the pillows for her. "I've settled the bill. That innkeeper wanted payment in advance," Mrs. Dunlap shook her head.

Polly replied, "Thank you for securing these rooms, Mrs. Dunlap. You've been so gracious to me."

Mrs. Dunlap shook a finger, "We were quite blessed to have arrived when we did, as immediately after I settled the bill, a rather worn group walked in the door and all asked for rooms. The innkeeper turned them away. There is only one vacancy left, the innkeeper said. The rest had to continue on in this dreadful night."

"To find another inn?" Polly asked as she situated herself in the bed.

Mrs. Dunlap's face betrayed a feeling of guilt crept over her, "I felt terrible that we had complained about our long journey by carriage, when they had an even longer one by ship!"

"Oh, Mrs. Dunlap..." Polly soothed.

"Well." Mrs. Dunlap said as she threw

her arms up helplessly, "Since we were already situated, I took pity on them and loaned them our carriage. I've just seen them off. Hoping to arrive at some church before the storm gathers up all its full fury." Mrs. Dunlap inhaled as she wandered toward Polly's window and looked out at the inky, rainy night, "Perhaps you should not have come with me to Meeting Town in your condition, Polly."

Polly explained, "I copied the document in English. I crafted the translation into German. I used my husband's vellum. I want to deliver it."

"Deliver it... Yes... now where..." Mrs. Dunlap mused.

"Well, if the people who were supposed to meet you are also lodging in this inn, then you can ask the innkeeper which rooms they occupy, can you not?" Polly asked.

Mrs. Dunlap gazed at the window pane as drop of water collected and formed rivulets streaking down the glass.

Mrs. Dunlap replied, "My husband got a letter from Mr. Livingston instructing me to meet with a Susanna Wright, yet the innkeeper said she has not returned to her room. Likewise, there was no note left for me..." Mrs. Dunlap sighed as she continued, "so, perhaps we can devise a plan to deliver it to the proper place in the morning."

The squeak of the Inn's sign, which hung beneath Polly's window, grew louder as it was tossed to and fro by the raging winds. Cries of pedestrians in the streets seeking shelter as they splashed in muddy puddles trying to get inside the nearest structure punctuated the sounds of pelting rains.

In the distance, Mrs. Dunlap noticed a faint glinting of dancing light through the window.

"I wonder what could be ablaze on a night like this?" Mrs. Dunlap shook her head, "Well, in case it gets brighter and disturbs your rest, I'll draw the window covers," Mrs. Dunlap concluded as she pulled the fabric along the pole over the window to cover the glass.

She turned to smile at Polly.

Mrs. Dunlap lit a candle to illuminate the room and rested the iron candlestick by Polly's bedside. The rain beat with greater intensity against the glass of the window pane.

"Mrs. Dunlap," Polly started as she bundled herself in a blanket, "This is the same Inn, in which Jane and her servants are lodged, yet I questioned the maid who walked me to this room. She had not seen them since breakfast."

Mrs. Dunlap saw Polly's crestfallen expression and rushed to her side to sit on the bed, "Oh, Polly. I understand how distressing this is for you. You are grieving for your husband just as you are on the precipice of having your first born child. Once we discovered that Jane Hargreaves was also staying at this Inn, I know how much you anticipated conversing with Jane. Perhaps she is having a warm supper with a new friend. All will right itself on the morrow at breakfast. Now, get some rest, Polly."

Mrs. Dunlap walked toward the door.

"Have pleasant dreams, Mrs. Dunlap," Polly forced a meek smile.

Suddenly, Polly winced with pain, "Oh! Mrs. Dunlap... I don't think this this can wait until morning."

Polly shut her eyes with such force, she saw spots. Polly gripped the sheets of her bed in reaction to the intense pain she felt.

Mrs. Dunlap rushed to her side. "Oh, Polly, I am unfamiliar with this region. I've just dispatched the carriage... and I do not know where to find a midwife. Polly, could you not perhaps master your wits and postpone this for when we return home?"

In response, Polly cried out.

Mrs. Dunlap, now atwitter, exclaimed, "Oh, how inconvenient... are you quite certain, Polly?"

"Yes!" Polly replied with labored breath, "Quite, Mrs. Dunlap," Polly shouted, "Quite Certain." Polly grabbed a small pillow and shoved it into her mouth, as saliva drenched the cotton encased feathers, which muffled her cries of pain.

With determined efficiency, Mrs. Dunlap swung open the guest bedroom door and closed it smartly behind her, securing Polly inside.

13 What Just Happened?

While at the coffee shop, the commotion not only disrupted the sipping patrons, but resulted in a foot-chase. Bryce, however, collared Primo Uomo, the opera singer Henry Mossop. Is Mr. Mossop innocent and falsely accused or is he somebody who has evaded justice is should get his comeuppance? It is in July and the hour to get the fractured colonies united to address the King of England is nearing, but so much could and has gone wrong.

With instinct and hunches to go on, the ladies knew that something had to be halted at the docks before a ship sailed.

Meanwhile, Button, now escaped from kidnappers, finds himself once again a captive. Can a "Good Samaritan" help Button? If successful, could this unknown Button's efforts contribute to the effort to defy the King of England and declare Independence? Collectively, our seemingly insignificant efforts just might add up to become a force to be reckoned with.

Henry Mossop presents his defense. Irish sailors add an interesting element to the mission. And Eliza Lucas, the one who improved on the way to produce Indigo Blue, takes charge.

But, Jane, it appears, has sadly fallen overboard. Polly, unaware, settles into the Inn, and has troubles of her own to contend with.

14 Did You Know...

This book presents the reader with a fictional character named Eliza Lucas. There was a real Elizabeth Lucas Pinckney who lived from 1722 to 1793.

This real-life Eliza was the oldest child of Lt. Colonel George Lucas, who served in the British Army. Eliza had two brothers, Thomas and George, and one sister, Mary (who was sometimes nicknamed Polly).

This fact about the real- Elizabeth was used as a back-story in the *Firebrand* series for the fictional Eliza. She was open to befriending the fictional Polly in the story since the real life Elizabeth may have had a sister nicknamed "Polly".

Also, it is rumored that one of the writers on the Wynter Sommers writing team had a cousin who had two daughters named Jane and Polly and that wove into the story, as well.

The real Elizabeth lived on a plantation in South Carolina where she did, in fact, refine her technique of producing an Indigo blue vegetable-dye. Eventually, this dye became an exportable good, and was very profitable prior to the Revolutionary War.

Some Colonists found that the currency they used was devalued.

The blue indigo dye blocks, however, some referred to as "blue gold" because that was used as a stable currency which maintained its value and served as a substitute currency when the colony needed stability.

Elizabeth experimented over the years to produce a crop of Indigo which would thrive in the Colonies, and in particular South Carolina.

By the end of the 17th century the cost to produce Indigo had dropped, making it more accessible and replacing woad in Europe. Woad is a yellow flowering plant which is another source of blue dye. I

Indigo was great to trade because it was very valuable. It provided blue dye which was applied to clothing, ink, and did not fade in color when applied to various fabrics. It was compact, easy to transport, and had a long shelf-life.

The Pinckney plantation made a fortune by being the largest producer of Indigo in Charles Town in the 1700's. With other Indigo producers, some say South Carolina exported about one million pounds per year.

The real Elizabeth married her long-time friend Charles Pinckney around 1744.

The real Elizabeth also researched for a cure for breast cancer. Many years later, in the 20th Century, Elizabeth "Eliza" Pinckney was inducted as the first woman into the South Carolina's Business Hall of Fame.

15 Vocabulary

In the early 1770s, before the colonies united into the United States of America, some words and terms were used, which may be explained in this section.

Divo/ Primo Uomo (pg 1) Divo is Italian for a prominent tenor. The form of the word assigned to a female is "Diva". Another term used to indicate a starring male singer is "Primo Uomo". The female version is "Prima Donna"....

Ingratiate To gain the favor of someone by being very nice.

Obnoxious Badly behaved, rude, offensive.

ABOUT Wynter Sommers

Wynter Sommers is the pseudonym for an American writing team, which harnesses multiple skills in technology, research, history and education. Formally trained with a PhD in Education, Wynter Sommers blends academic classroom experience, with corporate sophistication, and a passion for developing more effective student insights through engaging storytelling.

Wynter Sommers has a heart to inspire creativity and develop critical thinking skills, all to encourage readers to make wise choices in life.

Wynter Sommers takes each story and weaves the plot with classic gripping elements, which endure throughout repeated readings, revealing new meanings each time the story is explored. The small choices a reader makes in real life could have a lasting effect in future generations. This set of stories shows the origin of not just Bjorn Esterday and Sarah Paradise, but of their ancestors and the sort of world which was established, which unfolded in each generation until Bjorn and Sarah met.

It is rewarding to learn of heartfelt, thought provoking conversations taking place globally about the characters of these books. Should the reader be presented with extraordinary circumstances, it is the sincerest wish that they act with honor, truth and integrity to overcome obstacles in real life whilst the reader hones skills of self-reliance and collaborative teamwork despite barriers outside of the reader's control. Wynter Sommers hopes you enjoy the other **Bjorn Esterday Was not Born Yesterday** stories in this series.